KAREL

SUITE

FOR VIOLA AND PIANO
(opus 5)

AMP 8264

First Printing: April 2012

ISBN: 978-1-4584-2342-9

Associated Music Publishers, Inc.

DISTRIBUTED BY
HAL•LEONARD®
CORPORATION
7777 W. BLUEMOUND RD. P.O. BOX 13819 MILWAUKEE, WI 53213

First performance, 26 November 1946
Antonin Hyksa, viola,
Jiří Berkovec, Piano
Prague, Czechoslovakia

duration ca. 10 minutes

SUITE
for Viola and Piano
(opus 5)
1. Preludium

Karel Husa
(1945)

3

9

2. Elegie

Moderato

p molto cantabile

cresc. poco a poco

cresc. poco a poco

1

f

(cresc. poco a poco)

f secco

secco

dim. poco a poco

secco

poco a poco dim.

3. Marciale